BY LEA TADDONIO ILLUSTRATED BY ALESSIA TRUNFIO

LUCKY 8

#1 Welcome to Deadwood Hill

Spellbound

An Imprint of Magic Wagon
abdopublishing.com

To Jarah, Bronte and Poppy — LT

To my Family, my Love, my best friends and Eva. Thank you all
for helping me to make it real in all your personal ways. — AT

abdopublishing.com

Published by Magic Wagon, a division of ABDO, PO Box 398166,
Minneapolis, Minnesota 55439. Copyright © 2018 by Abdo Consulting
Group, Inc. International copyrights reserved in all countries. No
part of this book may be reproduced in any form without written
permission from the publisher. Spellbound™ is a trademark and logo
of Magic Wagon.

Printed in the United States of America, North Mankato, Minnesota.
092017
012018

**THIS BOOK CONTAINS
RECYCLED MATERIALS**

Written by Lea Taddonio
Illustrated by Alessia Trunfio
Edited by Heidi M.D. Elston
Art Directed by Laura Mitchell

Publisher's Cataloging-in-Publication Data

Names: Taddonio, Lea, author. | Trunfio, Alessia, illustrator.
Title: Welcome to Deadwood Hill / by Lea Taddonio; illustrated by Alessia Trunfio.
Description: Minneapolis, Minnesota : Magic Wagon, 2018. | Series: Lucky 8; Book 1
Summary: Twins Makayla and Liam move into a mysterious house - Deadwood
    Hill. To add to the mystery, they find a Magic 8 ball that appears to actually
    be magic. It sends the twins messages! Is the Magic 8 Ball helpful or
    haunted?
Identifiers: LCCN 2017946548 | ISBN 9781532130533 (lib.bdg.) | ISBN 9781532131134
    (ebook) | ISBN 9781532131431 (Read-to-me ebook)
Subjects: LCSH: Moving, Household--Juvenile fiction. | Ghosts--Juvenile fiction. |
    Mystery and detective stories--Juvenile fiction. | Brothers and sisters--Juvenile
    fiction.
Classification: DDC [FIC]--dc23
LC record available at https://lccn.loc.gov/2017946548

TABLE OF CONTENTS

CHAPTER 1

Number One Enemy

A black spider **DARTS** across my foot. "Oof!" I almost fall down the steep staircase. Grabbing the railing, I suck in a shaky breath.

My parents love that our new house is "historic." Mom said a **WITCH** lived in this exact same spot three hundred years ago.

The people in the town hung her from the oak tree next to our house. Afterward, the branch died. The **CREEPY** story is what gives the place it's name—Deadwood Hill.

Now that we've **MOVED** across the country, I guess it is also home sweet home.

Great.

But I have bigger things to worry about than **WITCHES** or SPIDERS. Tomorrow is the first day at my new school.

I walk in my bedroom and GAZE around at all the moving boxes. It's going to take forever to find the one that holds my video camera. It is my most PRIZED possession.

My dream is to be a famous director. I love **HORROR** movies.

The door **RATTLES**. I locked it when I came in for one reason. My brother, Liam, doesn't understand the meaning of the word *knock*.

"Go away!" I yell.

"Open up," Liam calls. "We need to talk."

"Too bad! I don't speak to **TRAITORS**."

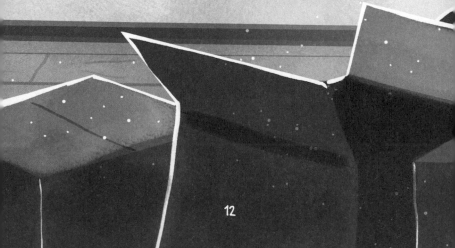

KEEP OUT!

14

My brother let me down. When Mom and Dad decided to *MOVE* for their jobs, Liam didn't complain. Not even once. I can't forgive him.

"Are you going to stay **MAD** forever?" Liam asks. "Remember what Mom always says. Every cloud has a *silver lining*. Maybe this move won't be so bad."

"Every silver lining has a CLOUD," I yell back. "*You* didn't have a best friend like Lucy. *You* weren't president of the school film club. But *you* went along with this *TERRIBLE* idea. Now get lost."

"But Makayla, I'm serious—"

"I am too." I glare around my creepy new bedroom, wishing for some of the Deadwood witch's MAGIC. I'd love to have the power to shoot fire out of my eyes. "Serious that you're my number one *enemy*."

CHAPTER 2

The Discovery

Two minutes later, Liam bangs at my window. He is sitting in the WITCH'S tree. There's something in his hand.

I'm a little impressed he's BRAVE enough to go near that creepy old tree.

Not that I'll tell him that.

"What are you doing out there?"
I ask. "Besides annoying me?"

"Let me in and I'll explain." His
eyes shine with EXCITEMENT.

I'm a tiny bit *curious*, so I crack
open the window.

He holds up a Magic 8 Ball
and talks to it. "This is my sister,
Makayla. She's nice, at least some
of the time."

"Please don't tell me your new hobby is talking to yourself," I snap. All I need is for my annoying brother to lose his mind.

"After lunch I explored the attic and made a **DISCOVERY**." His voice drops to a whisper. "One that's going to change our lives."

I stare at my brother without saying a word. Finally I say, "Is this a 'Make Makayla Feel Stupid' **TRICK**? Because I'm not in the **MOOD**."

"See for yourself." He shoves the Magic 8 Ball into my hands.

I **STARE** into the tiny plastic window. A white triangle **FLOATS** in water. Nothing happens.

"All right. That's it. I'm going back to ignoring you."

"*WAIT* a second, you'll see."

Slowly, the ball warms up. A soft light GLOWS from the round window.

"There!" My brother claps his hands. "See! What did I tell you?"

The triangle *twirls* faster and faster and then stops. I **GASP** when the words appear: *Welcome to Deadwood Hill.*

There is a **CRASH** as the ball drops from my hands.

CHAPTER 3

Here for Help

"You saw that, right?" Liam grabs the Magic 8 Ball off the floor. "Don't **TOUCH** that thing." I rush to the window. "**THROW** it out. Now. Get it out of here."

"Hey, guys!" my mom shouts from another part of the house. "I could use a little help."

"Wait, look!" Liam ignores Mom and passes me the Magic 8 Ball. My jaw falls OPEN. This time the triangle reads: *I'm here to help.*

"Hey. It's being *friendly*." Liam pats the side of the Magic 8 Ball. "I want to keep it."

"This isn't a pet hamster." I pace in front of the poster for my favorite movie, *Night of the Killer Vampire Wolves.*

There is a big difference between loving HORROR movies and living in one. "It could be a TRAP," I mutter.

"What do you mean?"

"How do we know this isn't an evil spirit who wants to *SUCK* us into a portal? Turn us into zombies?"

"Good point. How can we trust you?" Liam asks the 8 Ball.

"Quit talking to it! You're only encouraging. . ." my voice fades as the Magic 8 Ball **GLOWS** again.

This time the triangle reads: *Your camera is in a box by the bed.*

I walk to the box. **HOLDING** my breath, I open the lid. Sure enough, there is my camera. A chill runs up my spine.

CHAPTER 4

What If?

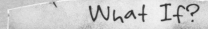

Liam and I both jump when Mom

BARGES into my room. Her hand

is on her hip.

"I've been CALLING

your names for five minutes. Come on,

you two. I need your help."

She grabs the Magic 8 Ball from

Liam. "Give that toy to me and let's go."

Liam and I exchange NERVOUS glances as we follow Mom downstairs. What's going to happen now?

"Hey, I used to have one
of these when I was a kid," she says,
shaking the Magic 8 Ball. "Will
my kids become better helpers?
Reply hazy, try again."

She **LAUGHS** and sticks it on a shelf.

"So **WAIT**," Liam grabs my arm. "When Mom uses the ball, it acts normal?"

My heart *beats* harder. "I think so."

"I'm waiting!" Mom yells from the living room.

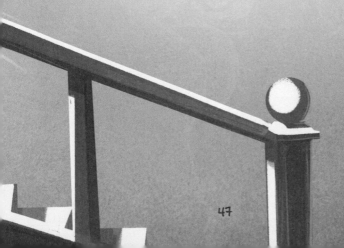

As we walk away, I can't shake the funny feeling that someone is **WATCHING** us.

Or some *thing*.

But two things are certain: There is a *secret* at Deadwood Hill. And I intend to **SOLVE** it.